E

D1317145

30735

This book
belongs to:

· ·

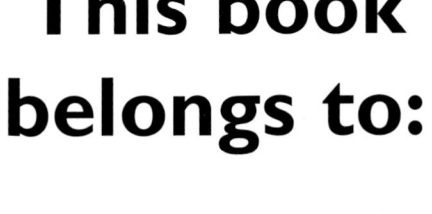

1. HUCKLE'S HOUSE
2. HILDA'S HOUSE
3. SGT. MURPHY'S
4. PIG FAMILY HOUSE
5. MR. FRUMBLE'S
6. FIRE STATION
7. TOWN HALL
8. MR. FIXIT'S HOUSE
9. BUSYTOWN HOSPITAL
10. SCHOOLHOUSE
11. MR. GRONKLE'S
12. SPROUT'S FARM

THE RECYCLING PLANT

BUSYTOWN AIRPORT

STADIUM

APRIL RHINO'S
HOUSE

THE PORT

MOUNT BUSY OBSERVATORY

SKI CHALET

Welcome to Busytown!

CAMPING GROUNDS

BUSY BAY POINT

BRUNO'S SNACK STAND

THE BEACH

THE TRAIN STATION

BUSYTOWN GRAND HOTEL

SEA FORT

First Aladdin Paperbacks edition April 1996
Copyright © 1995 by the Estate of Richard Scarry
Adapted from the animated television series *The Busy World of Richard Scarry*™
produced by Paramount Pictures and Cinar.
Aladdin Paperbacks
An imprint of Simon & Schuster
Children's Publishing Division
1230 Avenue of the Americas
New York, NY 10020
All rights reserved, including the right of
reproduction in whole or in part in any form
Designed and produced by Les Livres du Dragon d'Or.
Printed in Italy.
10 9 8 7 6 5 4 3 2 1
ISBN 0-689-80806-2

The Busy World of Richard Scarry

A Trip to the Moon

Aladdin Paperbacks

Benny Baboon, Harry Hyena, and Wolfgang Wolf are out looking for something good to eat. They walk past Mr. Fixit's workshop. Smoke rises from behind the roof.

"Look at all that smoke!" Harry exclaims. "Maybe there's something cooking! Let's go see!"

"Good morning, Mr. Fixit," Wolfgang says. "We saw the smoke and thought there might be something cooking."

"I have something cooking all right," Mr. Fixit replies, pointing aside. "It's my greatest invention ever! I'm building a rocket so I can go to the moon! Come. Have a look!"

"I wonder why Mr. Fixit wants to go to the moon?" Wolfgang whispers to the others.
"Maybe for something to eat!" Harry suggests. "I heard the moon is made of green cheese."
"Mmm!" Wolfgang dreams.
The three beggars enter the rocket to look around.

Just then, Huckle and Lowly walk up, pushing Huckle's bicycle.
"Good morning, boys," says Mr. Fixit. "Are you out for a morning ride?"
"We were," Huckle replies, "until I ran over a nail. My tire is flat."
"I can fix that in no time," says Mr. Fixit. "But first I need to finish my rocket ship."

"A rocket ship?" the boys wonder. "Wow!"
"Have a look around!" Mr. Fixit says,
inviting them inside.
The boys enter the rocket ship, amazed.

"I wonder what this does," says Huckle, reaching for a lever.
Luckily, Lowly stops Huckle's hand before he can touch it.
"Don't touch anything!" Lowly warns. "What if you accidentally sent us to the moon?"

"It would be **GREAT!**" replies Huckle. "We'd get to wear space suits."
Suddenly, three faces appear in the space suit helmets.
"Ahhh!!!" cry Huckle and Lowly.
"It's just us, boys!" Wolfgang says, walking over to them.

"Whew! We thought you were space monsters," says Huckle.
"There's no such thing as space monsters," Wolfgang says, laughing.
Just then, a hat flies in through the door. It lands at Wolfgang's feet.
"That looks like Mr. Frumble's hat!" Wolfgang says.

And here comes Mr. Frumble!
Look out! **OOPS!**
Mr. Frumble trips and bumps into
the lever, pushing it forward.

WHOOOSH! The rocket
door slides shut.
Lights begin to flash!
Dials spin! The rocket
begins to shudder
and rumble.
"What's going on?"
Lowly wonders.

"Look!" exclaims Wolfgang, pointing through the porthole. They all crowd around and see Mr. Fixit's workshop getting smaller and smaller. The rocket has taken off!
"Well, it works!" says Mr. Fixit on the ground, waving the rocket good-bye.

Inside, Mr. Frumble picks up his hat and starts for the door. "I will be on my way now," he says. "But you **CAN'T** leave, Mr. Frumble!" Huckle says. "This rocket is going to the moon!"

"Oh, then, in that case, I'll just wait over here," Mr. Frumble replies, sitting down on a chair. Soon he falls asleep and rises into the air!

Far from the earth's gravity, everyone in
the rocket has become weightless!
Wolfgang holds onto the steering wheel.
"Can you turn us around, Wolfgang?"
Harry asks.
"I don't know how to steer this thing,"
Wolfgang replies. "I don't even have a
driver's license!"
Outside, meteors appear through
the porthole.
"I don't think we're in Busytown any-
more," Lowly remarks.
The rocket ship whooshes about crazily.

Then, suddenly, it stops. **CRASH!** It has landed on the moon!
The steering wheel snaps off from the shock.
It is bent beyond repair.
"With this broken steering wheel, we will *never* get back home!"
says Wolfgang.
"How are we going to find a new one?" Huckle wonders.

They all decide to go explore the moon. Benny, Harry, and Wolfgang want to see if it really **IS** made of green cheese. Huckle and Lowly want to find something to repair the broken steering wheel. They all put on space suits and go outside. Mr. Frumble's hat decides to go out, too!

Huckle finds that riding his bicycle on the moon is great fun. With so little gravity, he can jump over an entire crater!

Suddenly, Huckle's bicycle handlebar comes loose.

"That's **IT!**" says Lowly. "I know how we can repair the rocket's steering wheel!"

The boys pedal back toward the rocket.
They pass the three beggars, who are tasting pieces of the moon.
"From the taste of it," says Wolfgang, "I'd say this green cheese has gone bad."
"You're right," adds Harry. "And it's as hard as rock!"
"Come on!" calls Huckle. "We're going home!"

Inside the rocket, Lowly has put the bicycle handlebar in place of the steering wheel.

Bravo, Lowly! That's a great idea!

"Ready to blast off when you are, Captain!" Lowly says to Wolfgang.

"I hope the rocket still works," Wolfgang replies.

"Has anyone seen my hat?" Mr. Frumble asks. The rocket starts to shake as Wolfgang pushes down on the lever. It rises slowly from the surface of the moon, then picks up speed.
"Whoaaaahhh!" they all shout.

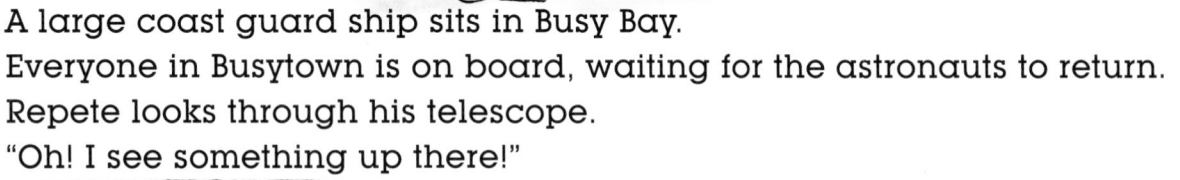

A large coast guard ship sits in Busy Bay.
Everyone in Busytown is on board, waiting for the astronauts to return.
Repete looks through his telescope.
"Oh! I see something up there!"

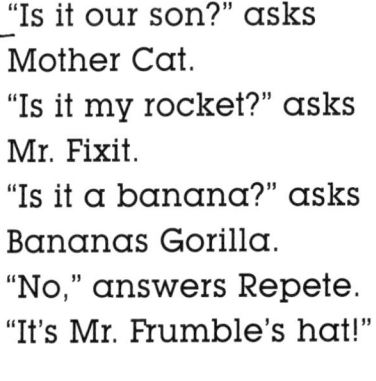

"Is it our son?" asks Mother Cat.
"Is it my rocket?" asks Mr. Fixit.
"Is it a banana?" asks Bananas Gorilla.
"No," answers Repete.
"It's Mr. Frumble's hat!"

"Then Mr. Frumble can't be far behind," Sergeant Murphy says.

SPLASH! The rocket falls into Busy Bay.

A helicopter flies toward the rocket and brings it safely back to the ship. Once on board, the rocket door opens and the six astronauts appear. Everyone cheers!
"May I leave now?" asks Mr. Frumble?

Mayor Fox prepares to hand out medals. "It is with great pride that I present these medals for bravery to Busytown's very first astronauts!" he says.

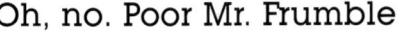

"Wolfgang Wolf, Harry Hyena, Benny Baboon, Huckle Cat, Lowly Worm, and ... and ... where is Mr. Frumble?" Over there, Mayor Fox! He's chasing his hat ... again! Look out, Mr. Frumble!

SPLASH!

Oh, no. Poor Mr. Frumble.

BUSYTOWN AIRPORT

THE RECYCLING PLANT

THE FLOUR MILL

STADIUM

APRIL RHINO'S HOUSE

THE PORT

PROPERTY OF
TRI-CITIES CHRISTIAN SCHOOLS
WESLEY CENTER